Sister Bear

A Norse Tale

adapted by **Jane Yolen**   illustrated by **Linda Graves**

MARSHALL CAVENDISH CHILDREN

For Alison Stemple, like Halva, a strong young woman living in the North.
Now all you need is a bear! And to WMIG, you wonderful illustrators,
whom I envy and love in equal measure.
—J.Y.

To my wonderfully creative father
—L.G.

Marshall Cavendish Corporation
99 White Plains Road
Tarrytown, NY 10591
www.marshallcavendish.us/kids

Library of Congress Cataloging-in-Publication Data
Yolen, Jane.
Sister Bear : a Norse tale / adapted by Jane Yolen ; illustrated by Linda Graves.
— 1st ed.
p. cm.
Summary: Halva is traveling with her trained bear to visit the king of
Denmark when they stop for the night at a cottage where, they learn, a pack
of trolls is about to make its annual Christmas Eve, causing trouble and
making a big mess. Includes author's note about the story's origins.
ISBN 978-0-7614-5958-3 (hardcover)   ISBN 978-0-7614-6072-5 (ebook)
[1. Folklore—Norway.] I. Graves, Linda Dockey, ill. II. Title.
PZ8.1.Y815Sis 2011   398.209481—dc22   [E]   2010024235

The illustrations are rendered in pastel, colored pencil, and watercolor.
Book design by Vera Soki
Editor: Robin Benjamin
Printed in China (E)
First edition
10 9 8 7 6 5 4 3 2

mc Marshall Cavendish
Children

❧ AUTHOR'S NOTE ❧

This story is adapted from Peter Christen Asbjørnsen and Jorgen Moe's *Popular Tales from the Norse*, published in an English translation in Edinburgh, Scotland, 1888. It can also be found in Dasent's *East o' the Sun and West o' the Moon,* New York: Dover, 1970 and as "The Christmas Visitors and the Tabby Cat" in Reidar Christiansen's *Folktales of Norway*, University of Chicago Press, 1964. Online the story is called "The Bear Trainer and His Cat" at http://www.pitt.edu/~dash/type1161.html and "The Cat on the Dovrefell" at http://www.sacred-texts.com/neu/ptn/ptn22.htm as well as at http://www.surlalunefairytales.com/authors/asbjornsenmoe/catdovrefell.html.

In all of the versions, it's a boy or man who has the bear, but I thought it was about time to show what a girl could do!

Asbjørnsen and Moe met at school as young teenagers. They shared a common interest in songs and legends and fairy tales. When Asbjørnsen made up his mind to become a collector of folktales, his friend Moe decided to work with him. They visited dozens of villages in Norway, writing down whatever they were told. In 1852 they published their first book of tales, some forty years after the Brothers Grimm had made retelling folktales popular in Europe.

The first Asbjørnsen and Moe book was so popular, their work ended up playing an important role in influencing the Norwegian written language.

There was a young girl named Halva up in Finnmark who found a white bear cub alone in the woods. She waited for almost a day to see if the mother would come for it, and when the bear did not, Halva wrapped the cub in her petticoat.

She took the cub home and asked
to keep it despite her mother and
father's misgivings.

"That bear will eat up
everything in the house, and
then eat us after," said her
mother. Her father agreed.

But the girl loved the cub, and it loved her back with all of its great heart.

Halva made the cub an embroidered coat, and it slept next to her bed at night. It ran by the side of her sleigh when she went out on the trail. And it never gave a bit of trouble.

In fact, the bear liked to dance on its hind legs to the music of Halva's wooden flute.

Every now and then, the bear would go out hunting on
its own, bringing home hare and ptarmigan for the family's
pot. So then even Halva's mother and father were impressed,
and they called it "Sister Bear."

Now when Sister Bear was big enough and strong enough, Halva decided to show her off to the king of Denmark, who liked remarkable things. So having gotten her parents' permission, Halva packed her sled with food for the journey, took her walking stick in hand, and off she went with Sister Bear down the snowy path.

The trees stood tall as sentinels, and the white bear jogged beside the sled.

They went along and went along and went along, and on Christmas Eve they came to a place called the Dovrefell.

Girl, sled, and bear pulled up beside a lonely cottage.

Halva knocked on the door, and it was opened by a grizzled man named Gusterson. She said, "Please, sir, do you have room in your shed for my reindeer and room at your fire for my bear and me tonight? I am taking her to show the king of Denmark, for she is a dancing bear."

Gusterson's jaw dropped halfway to his knees. "Alas," he said, "every Christmas Eve a pack of trolls comes down from the mountains. They party all night and all day here, leaving a horrible, stinking mess. My family and I are forced to leave or else be eaten by them."

"Oh, is that all?" said Halva. "That is no problem, for I can sleep in the side room and Sister Bear can lie down under the stove."

"Have you not heard a word I said? These are trolls. Ten feet high, green teeth, terrible manners."

"Sister Bear will take care of everything," said Halva.

The old man gave in, though not with any grace. "On your head, then!" he cried.

The Gustersons got everything ready for the trolls. The tables groaned with huge bowls of rice porridge and plump sausages, pots of fish boiled in lye. Then well before dark, the family fled the house. Halva didn't know where they planned to stay, but she was sure it would not be as fine as the house they were leaving.

"So now *we* must be the hosts," Halva said.

Sister Bear grunted in agreement.

Night came early on the Dovrefell, lit only by the flickering stars. And down the mountains, like giant shadows, marched the trolls, a huge family of them.

Some were so large their heads scraped the trees. Some were so small they were the size of pigs. Some had long twisty tails, and some had no tails at all. However, each one had a great long nose and great green teeth and breath that could fell an ox, had an ox been around to smell them.

The trolls set to eating and drinking everything in the house. They snorted and belched and made bad jokes. One of them even tried to sing. The others pelted him with hard rolls and leftover fishbones.

Silently, Halva watched it all from the side room. Then a little troll caught sight of the bear under the stove. He poked a fork against her nose, screaming, "Kitty, have some sausage!" The little troll thought the bear was a cat, since trolls are notoriously nearsighted. Again and again, he poked her until Sister Bear came out from under the stove and rose up on her hind legs, which made her taller than the largest troll.

"Leave her alone," cried Halva, running into the room, walking stick in hand. One of the trolls grabbed for Halva, but she eluded him and stood by the bear's side.

Several trolls began snarling and spitting, smelling like stink.

Halva's heart thudded in her chest, but Sister Bear didn't seem worried at all. Swatting the little troll who had poked her, she sent him flying into a pile of trolls at the table. This led the rest to squabble amongst themselves, and suddenly Sister Bear was upon them, snarling and growling.

"Roust them outside," called Halva, swinging her walking stick.

And that is just what Sister Bear did. Then she chased them all the way up one side of the mountain and halfway down the next.

Meanwhile, Halva put all the troll leavings in a big bowl for Sister Bear, keeping only a bit of sausage and one roll for herself. When Sister Bear returned, she ate and drank what Halva had salvaged for her.

The day after Christmas, when the Gustersons sneaked back to find a clean house, fresh food on the table, and a fine fir tree set up inside, Halva told them the story of how the trolls had been bested.

"Come next year," said Gusterson, "you and your bear."

"Thank you, we will," said Halva and shook his hand.

Then off went Halva with Sister Bear on the road to Denmark. Along the way they ran into the trolls, snorting and rooting around the forest. The biggest troll looked up. "Human girl, do you still have that cat with you?"

Halva smiled. "Why, yes, I have, sir." She was careful to be polite. One never knows with trolls.

"Will you two be at Gusterson's next Christmas?" His voice trembled like boulders rolling down the mountainside.

Halva laughed. "We've just accepted their invitation, along with the cat's two big kittens."

Sitting in the path, Sister Bear grinned, which showed off all her teeth. And my, didn't those trolls skidaddle out of there then!

A troll sigh blew out of the woods. "Oh, then," a deep voice called, "we'll never visit Gusterson's again."

Then Halva and Sister Bear walked all the way to Denmark.

The king was so pleased with the two of them, he loaded them down with gifts of embroidered cloth, gold rings and coins, and a special hat with places cut out for Sister Bear's ears.